the **BAD GUYS**

EPISODE

8

SUPERBAD

A SCHOLASTIC PRESS BOOK
FROM SCHOLASTIC AUSTRALIA

SCHOLASTIC PRESS
345 PACIFIC HIGHWAY LINDFIELD NSW 2070
AN IMPRINT OF SCHOLASTIC AUSTRALIA PTY LIMITED
(ABN 11 000 614 577)
PO BOX 579 GOSFORD NSW 2250
WWW.SCHOLASTIC.COM.AU

PART OF THE SCHOLASTIC GROUP
SYDNEY • AUCKLAND • NEW YORK • TORONTO • LONDON • MEXICO CITY
• NEW DELHI • HONG KONG • BUENOS AIRES • PUERTO RICO

FIRST PUBLISHED BY SCHOLASTIC AUSTRALIA IN 2018.
TEXT AND ILLUSTRATIONS COPYRIGHT © AARON BLABEY, 2018.

NATIONAL LIBRARY OF AUSTRALIA

A CATALOGUE RECORD FOR THIS
BOOK IS AVAILABLE FROM THE
NATIONAL LIBRARY OF AUSTRALIA

ISBN: 978-93-5275-635-3 (PAPER BACK)

TYPESET IN JANSON, ELO, KERBEROS FANG AND BEHANCE.
DESIGN BY NICOLE STOFBERG AND SARAH MITCHELL.

FIRST EDITION : 2019
THIS EDITION : DECEMBER 2022
PRINTED IN INDIA AT SANAT PRINTERS

· AARON BLABEY ·

the **BAD GUYS**

EPISODE **8** SUPERBAD

Well, if he *does* know, honey,
he doesn't seem to care . . .

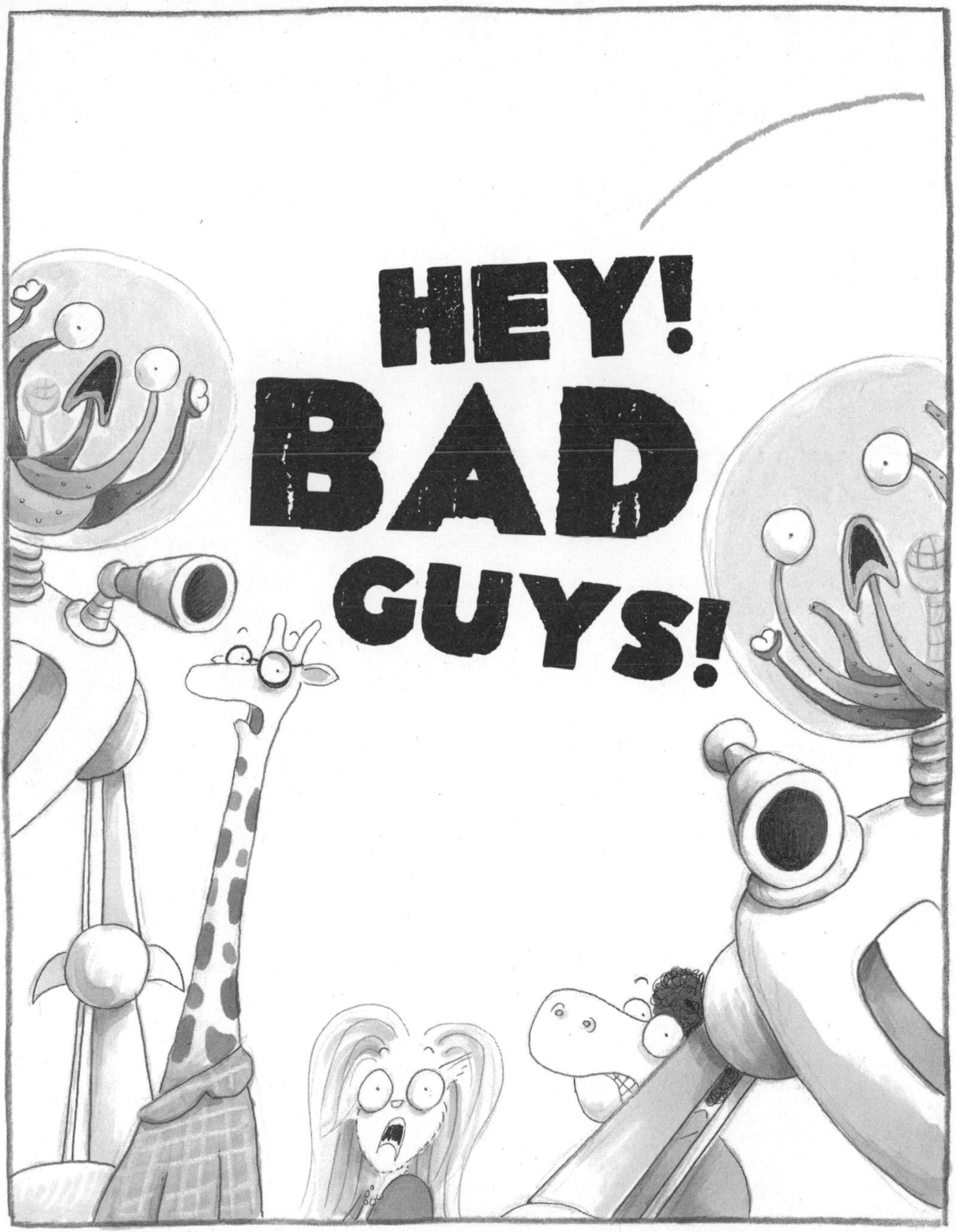
HEY! BAD GUYS!

· CHAPTER 1 ·
IDIOTS ASSEMBLE

It's the
GOOD GUYS CLUB!

Ah yes!
But we are developing a
better name that will sound
much cooler, señorita . . .

Get on with it, man . . .

Yes! Of course!
You've messed with the wrong
planet, hermanos.

SUPER SPEED . . .

 Oh, man.
He did it again.
He, like, ran straight
into that thing . . .

FoOOOOOF!

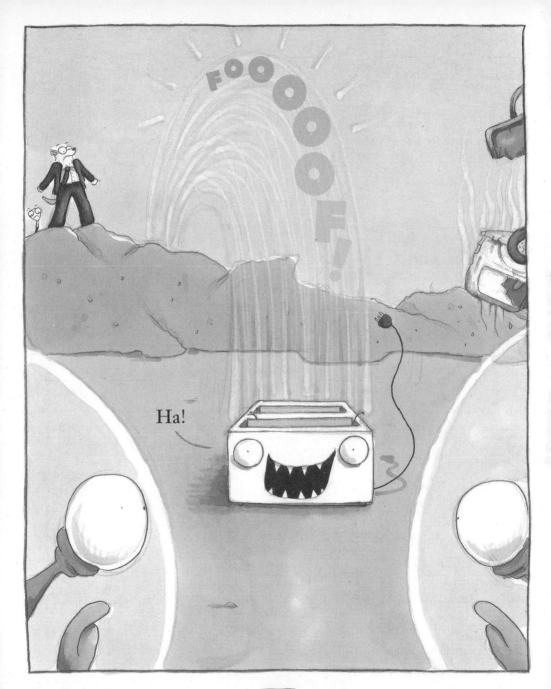

KER-CHINK!

Oh, no, no . . .
wait a minute . . .
hold that thought . . .

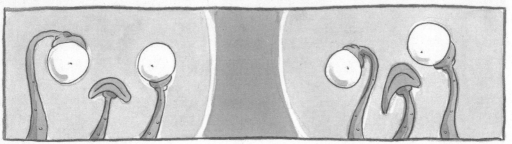

Aw, this is just embarrassing . . .

NO! These antics
have all been a
cunning trick to
distract you from
THIS!

FOOOOOOF!

Dude, you are SO
naked right now . . .

Mr Wolf!
WHAT ARE YOU DOING?!

Get in here!
ALL OF YOU!
RIGHT NOW!

ZAP!

ZAP!

BOOM!

BOOM!

BOOM!

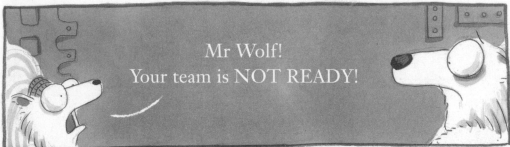

Mr Wolf!
Your team is NOT READY!

What makes you say that?

· CHAPTER 2 ·
THE LEAGUE

AGENT FOX

NAME: CLASSIFIED

PERSONAL HISTORY: CLASSIFIED

MASTER of SPYCRAFT

MASTER of MARTIAL ARTS

FLUENT in 14 LANGUAGES

PREFERRED VEHICLE: ANY

AGENT KITTY KAT

NAME: CLASSIFIED

PERSONAL HISTORY: CLASSIFIED

MASTER of MARTIAL ARTS

DOCTOR of MEDICINE

PILOT: FIRST CLASS

PREFERRED VEHICLE: AIRCRAFT

AGENT HOGWILD

NAME: CLASSIFIED

PERSONAL HISTORY: CLASSIFIED

DEMOLITIONS EXPERT

COMBAT SPECIALIST

PREFERRED VEHICLE: MOTORCYCLE

AGENT DOOM

NAME: CLASSIFIED

PERSONAL HISTORY: CLASSIFIED

COMPUTER HACKING GENIUS

DOCTOR of BIOLOGY, CHEMISTRY, PHYSICS, BIO-ENGINEERING + PHILOSOPHY

Meh.

AGENT SHORTFUSE

NAME: CLASSIFIED

PERSONAL HISTORY: CLASSIFIED

SPECIAL SKILLS: CLASSIFIED

That was so awesome.

I've seen better.

That video was so professional.

Why are we even here?

Because Fox has this crazy idea that you have potential.

But personally . . .

I don't have high hopes.

· CHAPTER 3 ·
WHAT'S GOING ON

Welcome to our
SECRET HEADQUARTERS.
Now you know a little bit about us,
so let's talk about **YOU.**

Mr Wolf, Mr Snake, Mr Shark and Mr Piranha—
the International League of Heroes is
well aware of your recent work and
we've all been briefed on your . . .
NEW TALENTS.

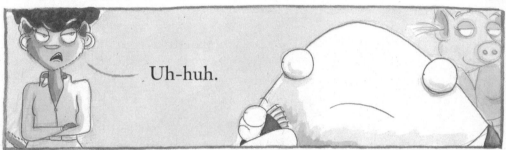

I'd also like to introduce my team to another very special member of the Good Guys Club—

LEGS!

Legs?
Are you OK?
You don't seem
your usual,
cheerful self.

Huh?
Yeah.
I'm fine.
Just FINE.

He likes to be called Mr Tarantula!

Ah! Sorry, Mr Tarantula . . .

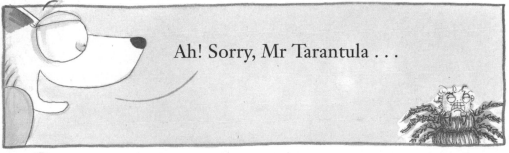

Yeah, yeah,

WHATEVER!

O . . . K . . .

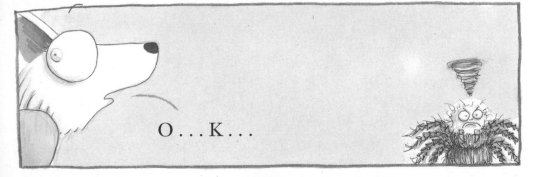

It's the weirdest thing . . .
I just got you a muffin.

Aw, thanks!

And finally, the . . . er . . . newest
member of the Good Guys Club—

MILTON.

And yes, in case you're wondering,
Milton *does* appear to be a **DINOSAUR**
from the Cretaceous period . . .

A dinosaur with an IQ of **512.**
According to my tests, he's easily the **MOST INTELLIGENT BEING ON THE FACE OF THE EARTH.**

Does anyone want to explain that?

It's kind of creeping me out . . .

Oh you're making me blush, dear lady—*really!*

What's a few hundred IQ points between friends? I'm just thrilled to be involved, and I must say, you all seem *lovely*.

Who'd care for a cup of tea?

Yep, that just happened.

Seriously, am I the only one creeped out by him?

Sooooo, obviously something highly unusual happened to all of you when you passed through that **VORTEX**.

Milton became **HYPER-INTELLIGENT...**

I really like her. She's *delightful*, don't you think?

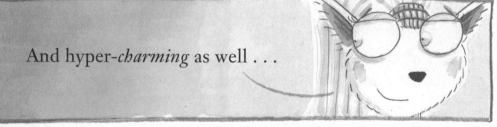

And hyper-*charming* as well . . .

On the other hand, Mr Piranha has

SUPER SPEED.

Mr Shark can

SHAPE-SHIFT.

Mr Snake has rather remarkable

MIND POWERS . . .

What*ever.*

Oh, sorry.
Did I touch
a SORE
SPOT?

I don't
know what
you're
talking
about.

Look, here's another one . . .

POKE!

Oh wow.
So many sore spots . . .

POKE!

POKE!

POKE!

Yeah, yeah.
Run away, 'Mr Remarkable'.
I've got my eye on you.

And as for

MR WOLF . . .

Aw, he's just a good old-fashioned **NUDIST!**
You looked FINE out there today,
baaaybeeee . . .

Keep it nice, Agent Hogwild.

As we all know, Mr Wolf has

SUPER STRENGTH.

Hey! Why are you holding
a trumpet, chico?

Now ain't YOU a cutey . . .

Gulp!

Unfortunately though, there's a **PROBLEM.** Other than Milton, none of you are able to fully **CONTROL** your powers . . .

I'VE GOT POWERS! I DO! AND I *CAN CONTROL THEM!* LOOK! I'VE GOT **CRAZY SPIDER POWERS...**

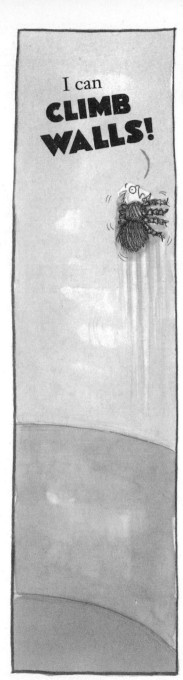

Ahhh . . . I think that's just called **'BEING A SPIDER'** isn't it?

Yeah, buddy. It kind of is.

But that's why we LOVE YOU, chico! You're just the **SAME OLD MR TARANTULA!**

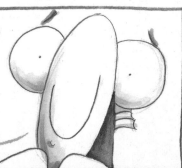

WHY DIDN'T I GET SUPERPOWERS?!

Ohhh, THAT'S why you're grouchy . . .

I'M NOT GROUCHY!

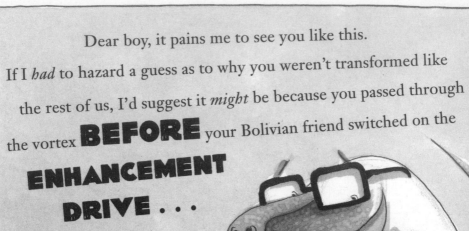

Dear boy, it pains me to see you like this.

If I *had* to hazard a guess as to why you weren't transformed like the rest of us, I'd suggest it *might* be because you passed through the vortex **BEFORE** your Bolivian friend switched on the **ENHANCEMENT DRIVE . . .**

HOW *DARE* YOU!
I didn't switch on ANYTHING!

Are you certain?
It was probably marked
'DO NOT PRESS' or
something like that . . .

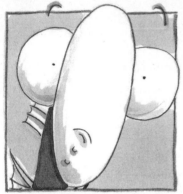

Look!
A cloud shaped
like a peanut . . .

You like peanuts?
Why don't we go out tonight and
get a whole crate of peanuts?

That sounds like **FUN.**
I bet you're a
good dancer, too.
Wanna go dancin'?

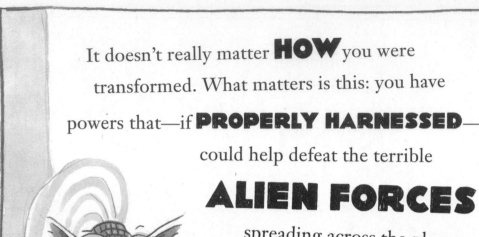

It doesn't really matter **HOW** you were transformed. What matters is this: you have powers that—if **PROPERLY HARNESSED**—could help defeat the terrible

ALIEN FORCES

spreading across the planet.

I cannot lie, the situation is not looking good . . .

Their **MOTHERSHIPS** have settled above every major city . . .

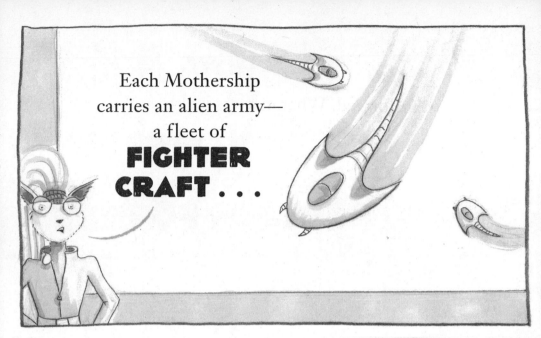

Each Mothership carries an alien army— a fleet of **FIGHTER CRAFT** . . .

and a legion of **ROBOT WAR MACHINES** used by the aliens on the ground.

The aliens are able to

CHANGE THEIR SIZE AT WILL.

They can be gigantic one minute and then shrink down to

fit inside the helmet of a **WAR MACHINE.**

That's how **MARMALADE**

disguised himself as a guinea pig.

They are HIGHLY ADVANCED.

They are HOSTILE.

And they are **EVERYWHERE.**

Well in that case, I'd better put my **ENORMOUS BRAIN** to work and come up with a **PLAN.**

BUT!
I'll need an assistant!
And there's only one name
at the top of my list—
MR TARANTULA,
I need you!
I suspect you're more
important to our survival
than you think . . .

Yeah, OK,
*what*ever . . .

Goodness!
I've just realised
you are entirely
without trousers!

Yeah, well, get over it . . .

And as for the rest of you . . .

· CHAPTER 4 ·
BE A TEACUP

Lesson One—
DON'T ANNOY ME.

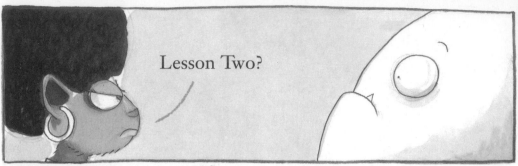

Lesson Two?

Be a teacup.

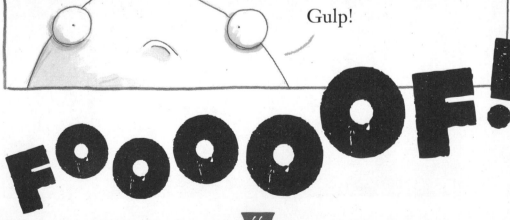

Gulp!

FOOOOOOF!!

But can you be a teacup . . .

when it matters?

SSSSSSSSSSS!

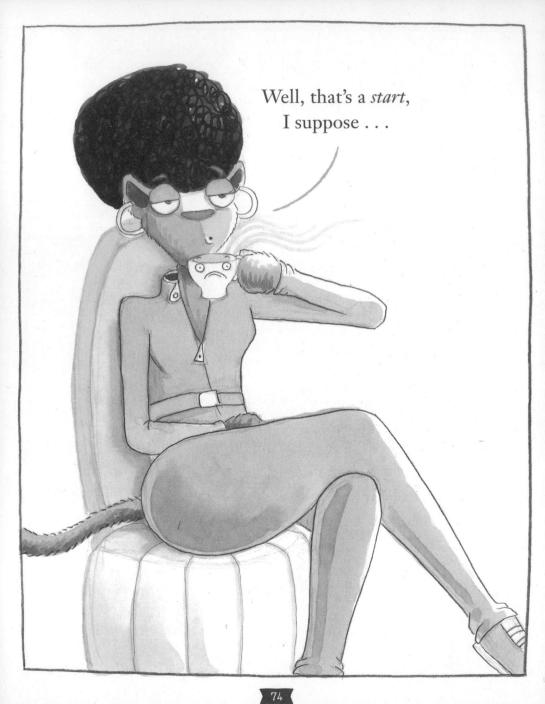

· CHAPTER 5 ·
TURN! TURN! TURN!

What's going on here?!
Why are we in this
TINY METAL ROOM?

Well . . . we're
going to play
a **GAME.**

Oh . . . OK . . . I like games.
What kind of game?

It's my favourite.

Really? What's it called?

KISS
CHASEY

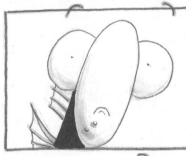

I'm sorry, it sounded
like you said . . .

You **RUN . . .**

I **KISS!**

Listen, baby, I could do this ALL day.

But we're in a bit of a rush, and you
have to stop crashing into walls,
so we need to take this to the

NEXT LEVEL . . .

Ready?

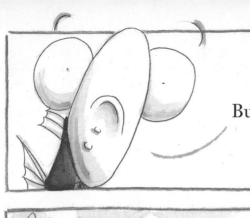

But I'll be a little fish-kebab!

You think I'd let that
happen to you?
I *believe* in you, sweet cheeks.
All you have to do is

TURN.

I KNOW you can do it.

But just in case . . .

give me a great, big
GOODBYE KISS.

· CHAPTER 6 ·
THE
BAD GIRLS

Yeah.
Well, I've seen better.

Oh sure.
Anyone can lift a **FRIDGE,**
a **CHAINSAW** and a
SECRET AGENT
off the ground using only their
MIND . . .

So . . . why don't we get Agent Fox to sing a little opera . . .

GRRRRRING!

GRRRRRRING!!

And let's start up that chainsaw . . .

YAWN

Oh, c'mon!
That was *awesome!*

Hey Fox? Can you take over?
Mr Remarkable's cheap tricks
are really bumming me out.

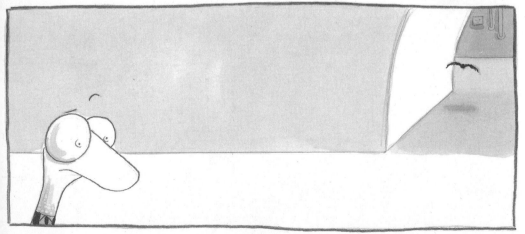

Why does she have to be so **NEGATIVE?**

Why do you think we call her **'AGENT DOOM'?**

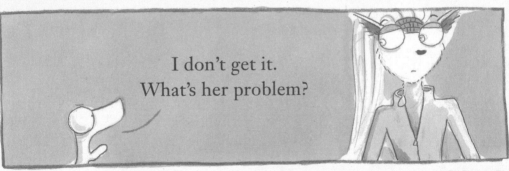

I don't get it. What's her problem?

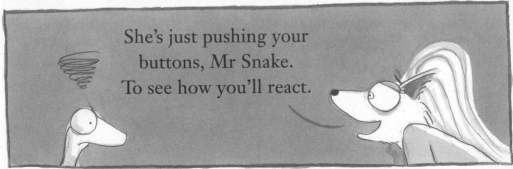

She's just pushing your buttons, Mr Snake. To see how you'll react.

Yeah, I get it.

YOU SUPER-SHINY-HERO-LADIES

think we're NOTHING don't you?

We're just a bunch of dirty crooks, right?

You don't think we've got what it takes.

None of you do.

But let me tell you something—

You don't know me AT ALL.

YOU KNOW

NOTHING

ABOUT ME.

Wow.

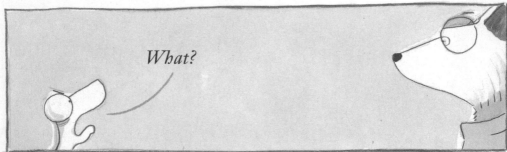

What?

You STILL don't get it, do you?

Get WHAT?!

Where I come from,
they **HUNT** foxes, Mr Snake. For fun.
Because they think we're worthless,
dirty thieves who don't deserve to live.

When I was young . . .

I lost everything.

Well, they told her early on that she couldn't be on the playground with the other kids because she was **'JUST A DANGEROUS ANIMAL'**.

Eventually, that made her pretty angry too.

And **AGENT HOGWILD**
was *told* her whole life she was bad.
So guess what?
She started *acting* like she was bad.

AGENT DOOM
was picked on every single day
for being a 'creepy weirdo' . . .

And nobody even
wanted to go near
AGENT SHORTFUSE.
Ever.

But then, somehow, we found each other.

And we made a pact.

We decided to take all our hurt and our anger and our fear and turn it all into something **GOOD.**

Instead of trying to hurt those who'd hurt us, we started trying to **PROTECT THOSE WHO CAN'T PROTECT THEMSELVES.**

So, don't you see, Mr Snake?

We *are* you.

· CHAPTER 7 ·
THE FINAL EXAM

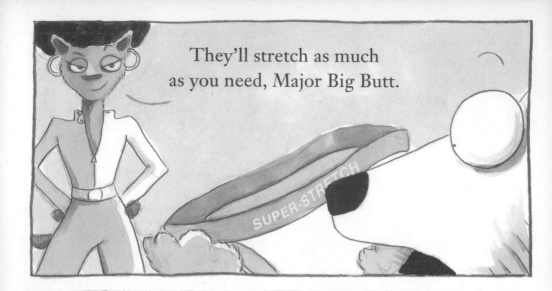

They'll stretch as much as you need, Major Big Butt.

SUPER-STRETCH

Put them away for now though, Mr Wolf. You guys have something you need to do first . . .

MOMENTS LATER . . .

Huh?

This is your
FINAL TRAINING EXERCISE.
It's simple—*put Agent Shortfuse in the box.*
Good luck, gentlemen.

Oh man, I was worried there for a second. OK, Agent Shortfuse, we can do this the **EASY WAY** or—

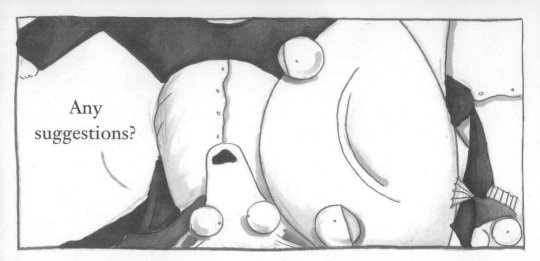

Any suggestions?

I'm trying to **HOLD HER WITH MY MIND** but she takes me out before I can focus.

She's too fast and too strong. None of us can take her **ALONE.**

Ready?

In your face,
Shortfuse!
You can't catch me!

And
while he
distracts
her . . .

· CHAPTER 8 ·
A MARVELLOUS PLAN

OPERATION TARANTULA

Ladies and gentlemen, I have developed a **PLAN** to give us the upper hand in this struggle against the Alien Forces. I call it—*Operation Tarantula!*

No offence, but you've named it after the only guy without superpowers?

Really?

WE don't have 'superpowers'. You got a problem with THAT?!

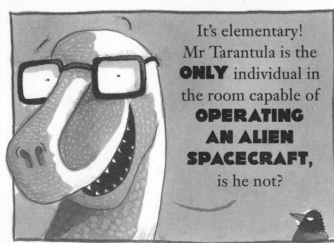

It's elementary! Mr Tarantula is the **ONLY** individual in the room capable of **OPERATING AN ALIEN SPACECRAFT,** is he not?

That's not true. I could *totally* do it.

And **OPERATION DOOM** would sound totes cooler.

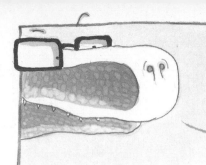

Hmmm. But are you small enough to sneak into the control deck of the Mothership **WITHOUT BEING NOTICED?**

NO! YOU ARE *NOT!*
The **ONLY** way we can stop this invasion is to take charge of a Mothership and turn it against them.
Therefore! The mission is to

SNEAK MR TARANTULA ON BOARD,

any way we can.

But what about all the aliens **ON BOARD?** Who will protect Legs? He can't go in there alone . . .

Oh no, dear boy. He won't be alone . . .

Yeah . . . that could work.

Sounds good to me.

MY TEAM will take on the aliens here on the *ground*. We'll keep them off you as long as we can.

Mr Wolf?
Your team needs to get

AGENT SHORTFUSE
and **MR TARANTULA**
onto that **MOTHERSHIP.**

· CHAPTER 9 ·
BIG TROUBLE

This is it,
Mr Wolf.

Are you OK?

I . . .
I just feel a little . . .

You'll do *great*.

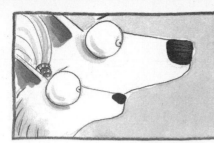

Man.
You two are
something else.

But you know what?

We wouldn't last
five minutes without you.

Z¡ZZZ**ZZZZ!**

MR WOLF?!

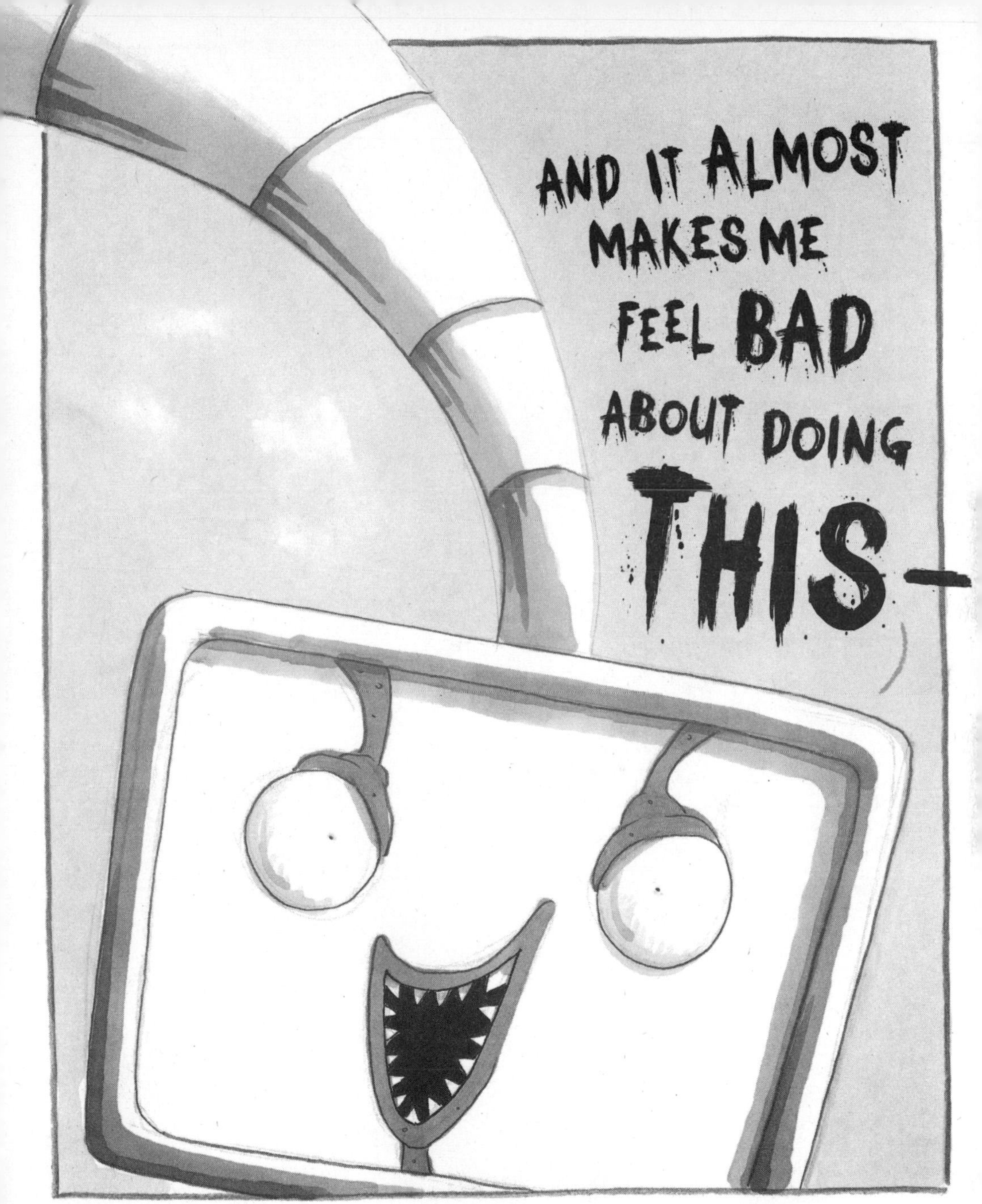
AND IT ALMOST MAKES ME FEEL BAD ABOUT DOING THIS–

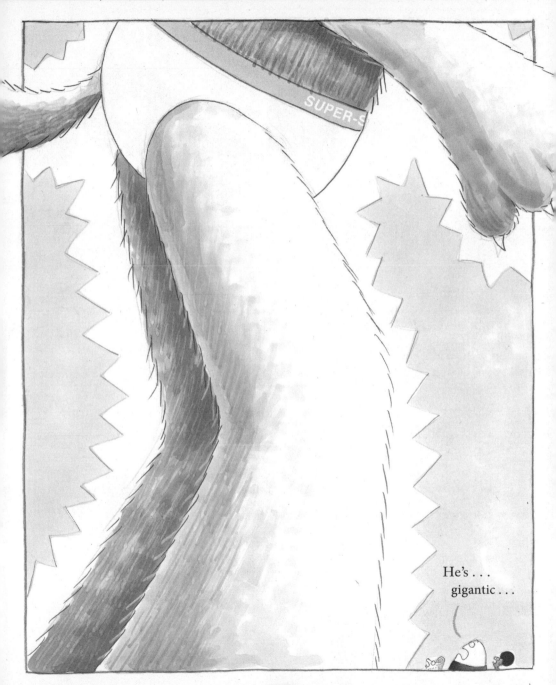

The Three Little Pigs were *right?!*

the **BAD GUYS** EPISODE **9**

COMING SOON . . .

TO DESTROY YOUR TOWN.